ZONDERkidz | I Can Read!™

BEGINNING READING 1

Sheerluck Holmes and The Case of the Missing Friend

story by Karen Poth

It was a foggy night
in London.

Dear Parent:
Your child's love of reading starts here!

Every child learns to read in a different way and at his or her own speed. You can help your young reader improve and become more confident by encouraging his or her own interests and abilities. You can also guide your child's spiritual development by reading stories with biblical values and Bible stories, like I Can Read! books published by Zonderkidz. From books your child reads with you to the first books he or she reads alone, there are I Can Read! books for every stage of reading:

SHARED READING

Basic language, word repetition, and whimsical illustrations, ideal for sharing with your emergent reader.

BEGINNING READING

Short sentences, familiar words, and simple concepts for children eager to read on their own.

READING WITH HELP

Engaging stories, longer sentences, and language play for developing readers.

READING ALONE

Complex plots, challenging vocabulary, and high-interest topics for the independent reader.

ADVANCED READING

Short paragraphs, chapters, and exciting themes for the perfect bridge to chapter books.

I Can Read! books have introduced children to the joy of reading since 1957. Featuring award-winning authors and illustrators and a fabulous cast of beloved characters, I Can Read! books set the standard for beginning readers.

A lifetime of discovery begins with the magical words "I Can Read!"

Visit www.icanread.com for information on enriching your child's reading experience.
Visit www.zonderkidz.com for more Zonderkidz I Can Read! titles.

A friend loves at all times.
He is there to help when trouble comes.
— Proverbs 17:17

ZONDERKIDZ

Sheerluck Holmes and The Case of the Missing Friend
©2014 Big Idea Entertainment, LLC. VEGGIETALES®, character names, likenesses and other indicia are trademarks of and copyrighted by Big Idea Entertainment, LLC. All rights reserved.
Illustrations ©2011 by Big Idea Entertainment, LLC.

This title is also available as a Zondervan ebook.
Visit www.zondervan/ebooks.

Requests for information should be addressed to:

Zonderkidz, 3900 Sparks Drive, Grand Rapids, Michigan 49546

ISBN 978-0-310-74171-8

All Scripture quotations, unless otherwise indicated, are taken from The Holy Bible, *New International Reader's Version®, NIrV®*. Copyright © 1995, 1996, 1998 by Biblica, Inc.® Used by permission. All rights reserved worldwide.

Any Internet addresses (websites, blogs, etc.) and telephone numbers in this book are offered as a resource. They are not intended in any way to be or imply an endorsement by Zondervan, nor does Zondervan vouch for the content of these sites and numbers for the life of this book.

Editor: Mary Hassinger
Art direction: Karen Poth
Cover design: Ron Eddy
Interior design: Ron Eddy

Printed in China

Sheerluck Holmes
and Bobby Watson
went for a walk.

"Stop!" shouted a policeman.

Sheerluck jumped.

He swallowed some bubbles

from his pipe.

"Sniffy is gone,"
the policeman said.
"Come quick!"

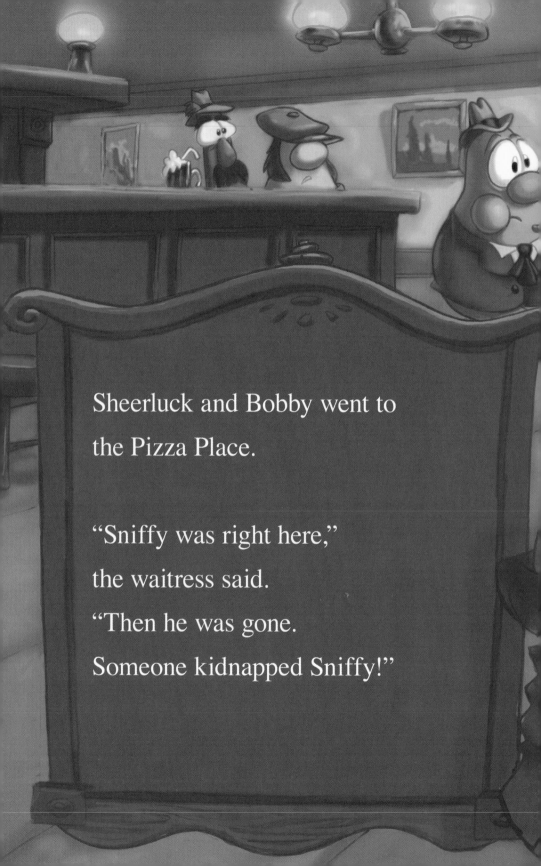

Sheerluck and Bobby went to
the Pizza Place.

"Sniffy was right here,"
the waitress said.
"Then he was gone.
Someone kidnapped Sniffy!"

"I know what happened here,"
Sheerluck said.

"Sniffy ran away."

"How do you know?" Watson asked.

"I read the sign," Sheerluck said.
"Someone hurt Sniffy's feelings.
But who?"

It was a mystery!

Sheerluck started asking questions.

"Did YOU hurt Sniffy's feelings?"

he asked Morty.

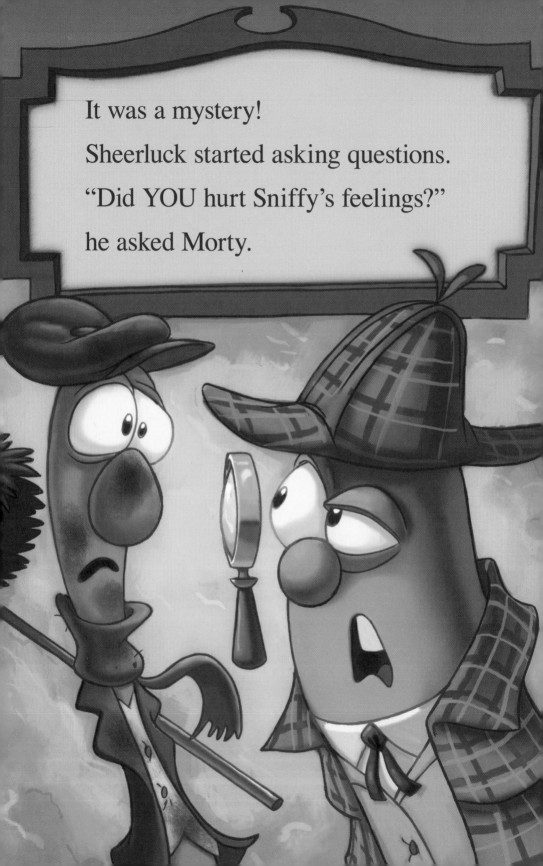

SLAM

Suddenly the lights went out.
It was very dark.

CRUNCH

Then Sheerluck asked Nommy,
"Did you hurt Sniffy's feelings?"

Then Sheerluck asked Percy,
"Did you hurt Sniffy's feelings?"

And then he asked Jerry
and the policeman.

Each one said,
"I didn't do it."

SLAM, BANG, CRUNCH!

Veggies shouted and pushed.

17

CLICK!

The lights came back on.

Veggies were piled by the door.

"I turned off the lights," said Watson.

"I knew the one who hurt Sniffy's

feelings would try to leave."

"Did you ALL hurt

Sniffy's feelings?"

Sheerluck asked.

"I think we did,"
Nommy said.
"Sniffy was on our dart team."

"It was Sniffy's turn to throw,"
said Percy. "He sneezed.
His dart hit the floor.
We lost the game."

"We all got mad," the Veggies said.
"Sniffy wrote that note.
Then he ran away."

"We have to find him!"

Nommy said.

"He's out there all alone!"

The group followed Sniffy's footprints.

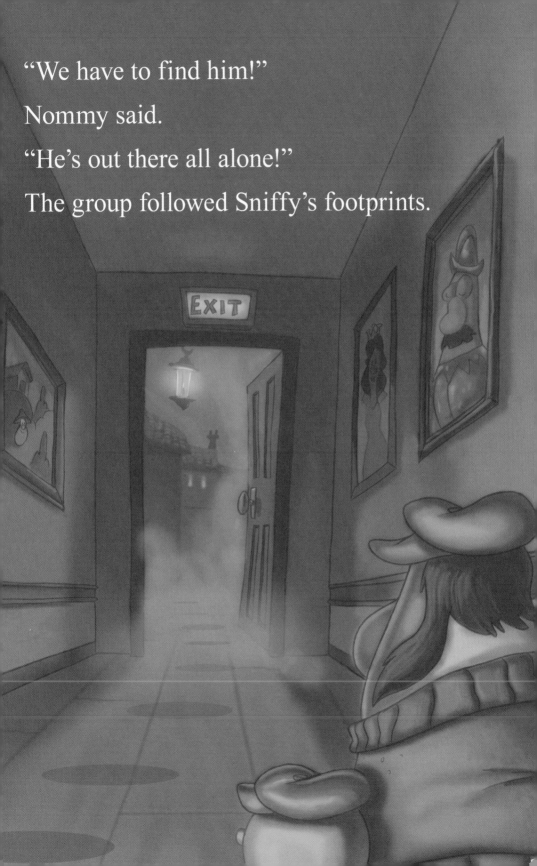

Everyone ran outside.

It was foggy.

It was dark.

They heard dogs howling.

"Oh no!" Nommy yelled.

"The dogs have him!"

The dogs ran to Sniffy.

They were all over him.
They were licking him!

"We're sorry," Nommy said.

"We didn't mean to hurt your feelings."

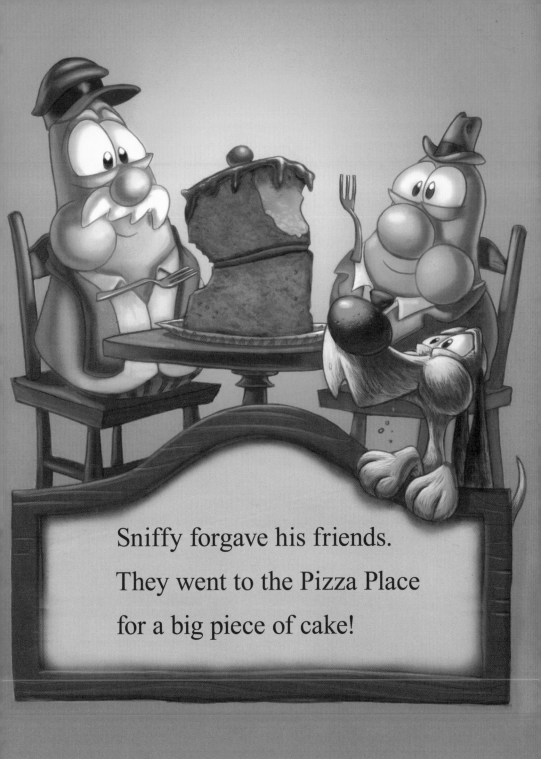

Sniffy forgave his friends.
They went to the Pizza Place
for a big piece of cake!

Everyone was happy.

"Mystery solved,"

Sheerluck said.

"And a lesson learned!"
the policeman said.

"That's right," agreed Sheerluck.
"We should always be kind to others!"

Watson and Sheerluck

left the Pizza Place.

The fog was gone.

It was a beautiful night in London.